I Want a Pet

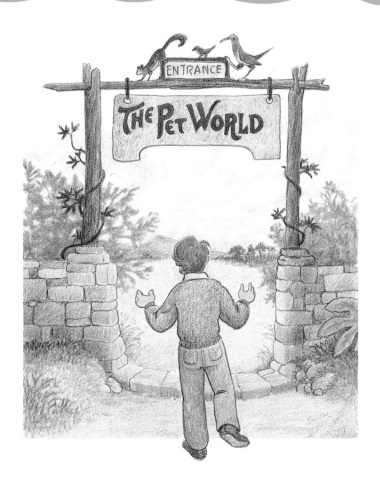

Written by
Barbara Gregorich
Illustrated by
Rex Schneider

I want a pet.

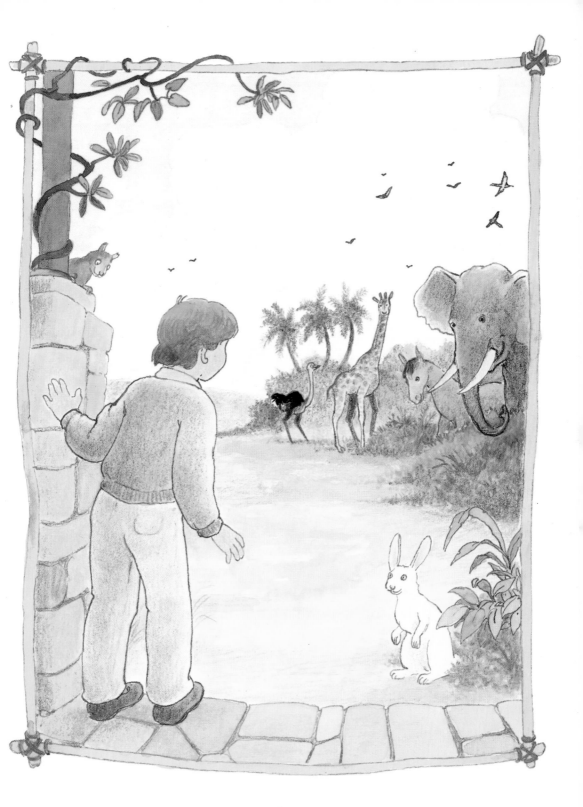

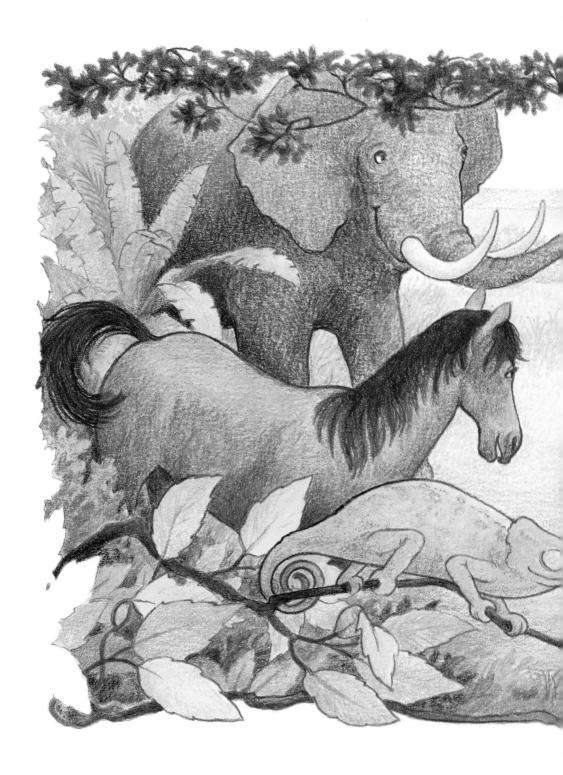

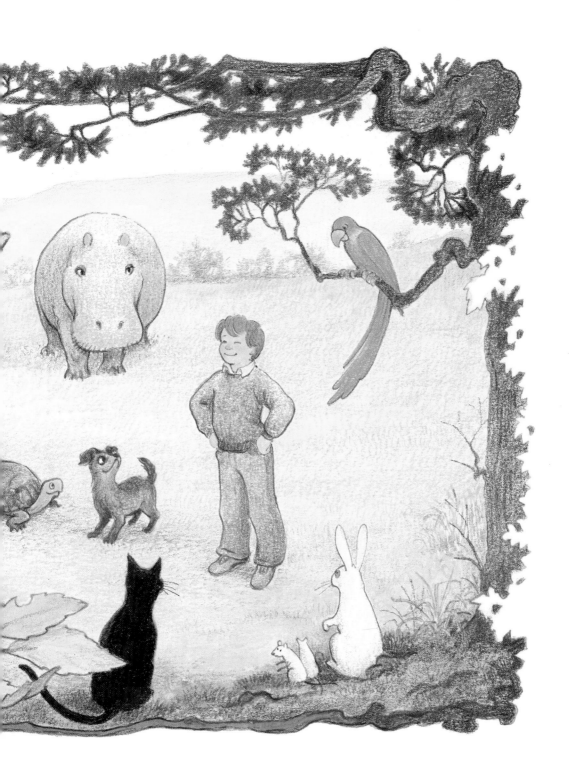

I do not want a very big pet.

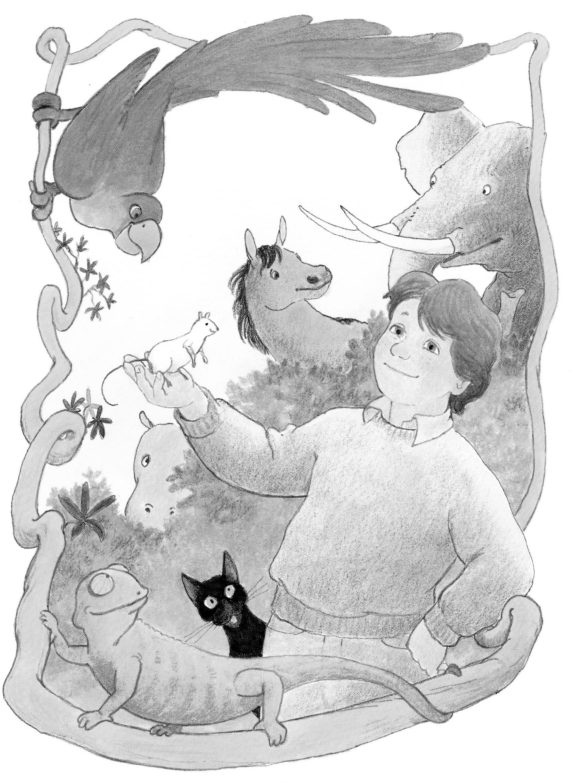

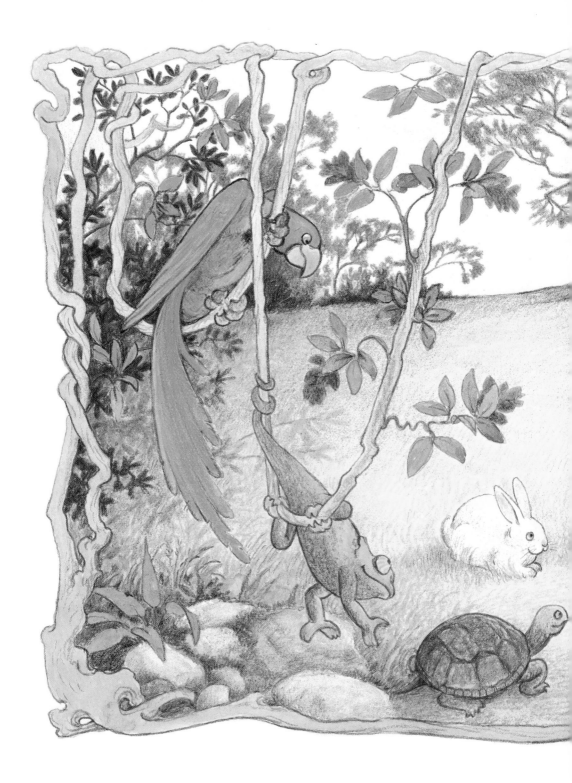

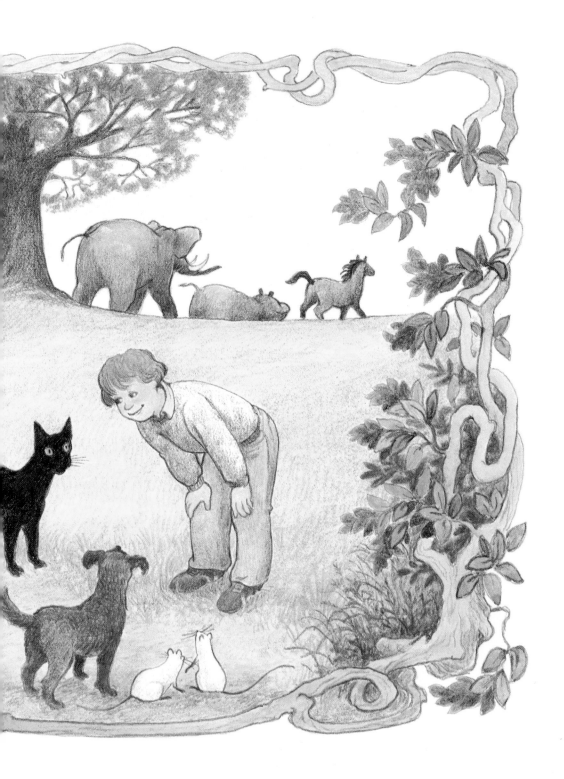

I do not want a brown pet.

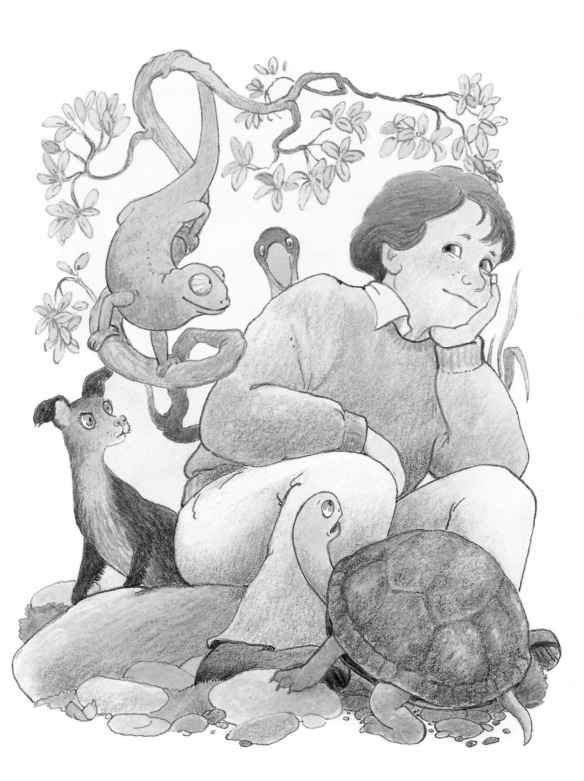

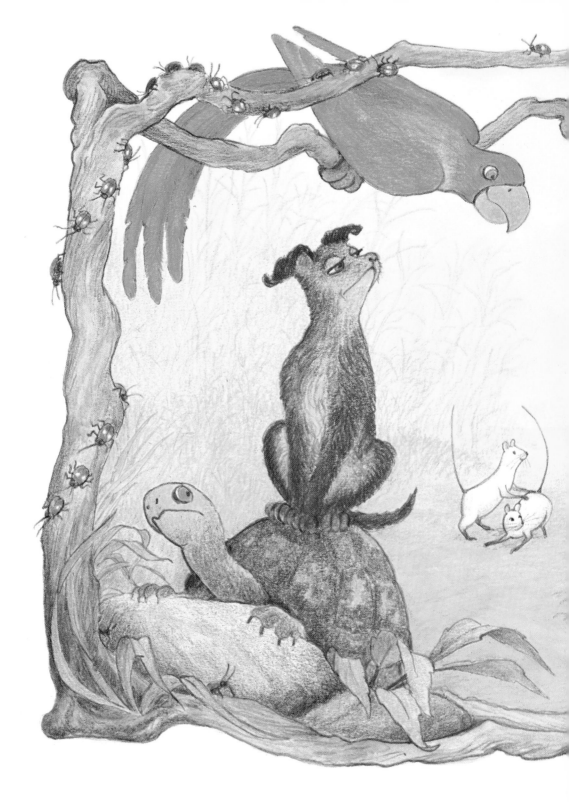

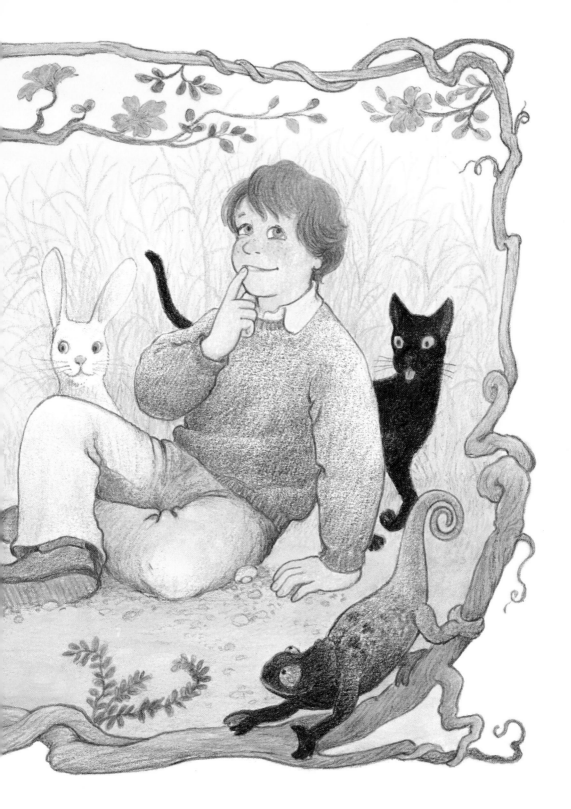

I do not want a black pet.

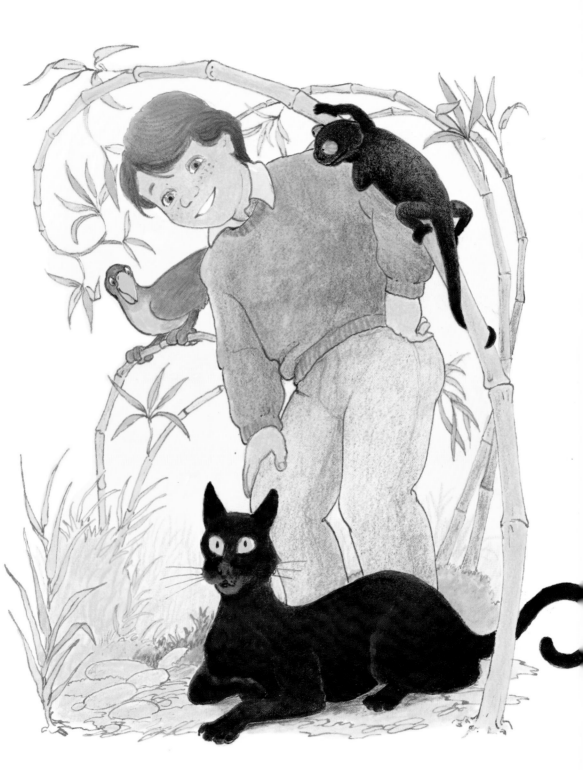

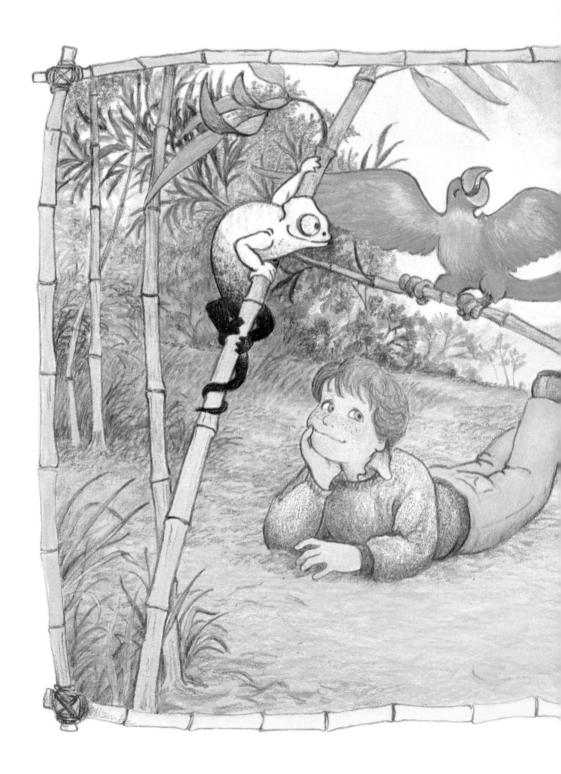

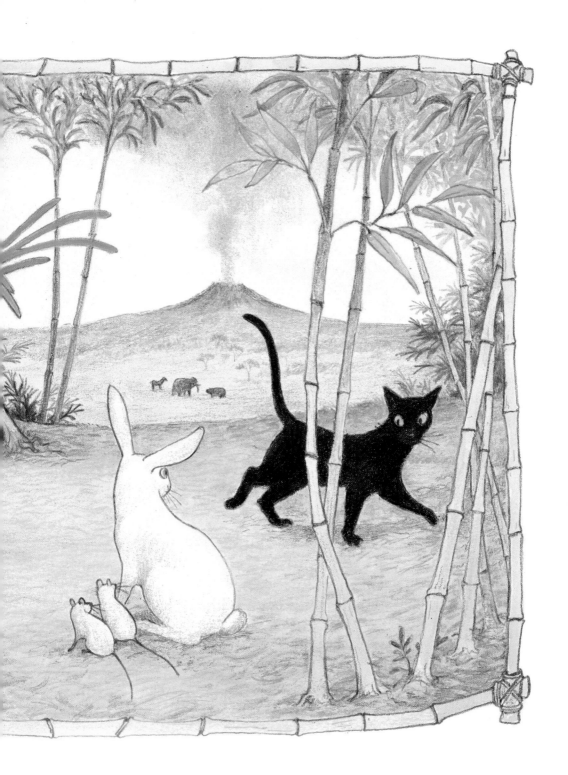

I do not want a white pet.

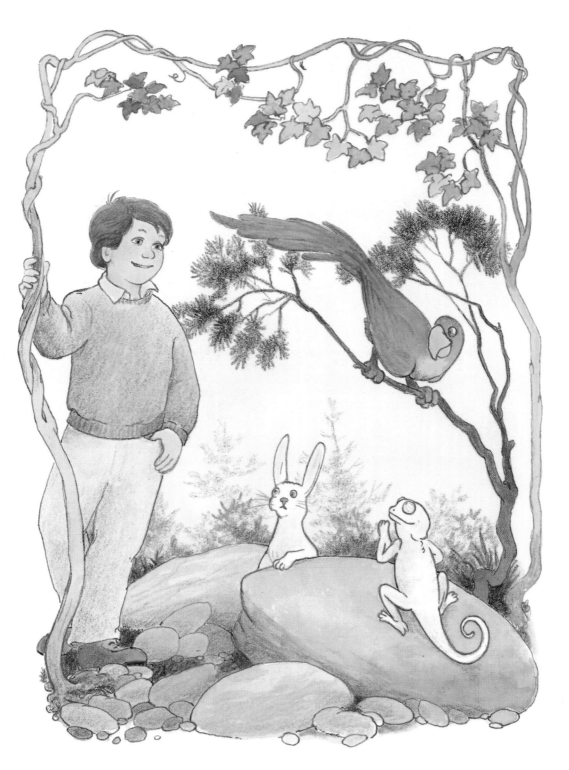

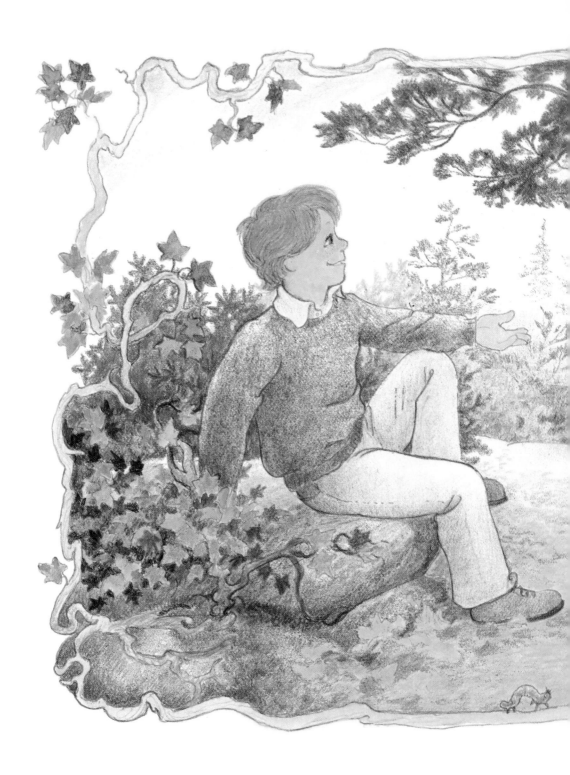

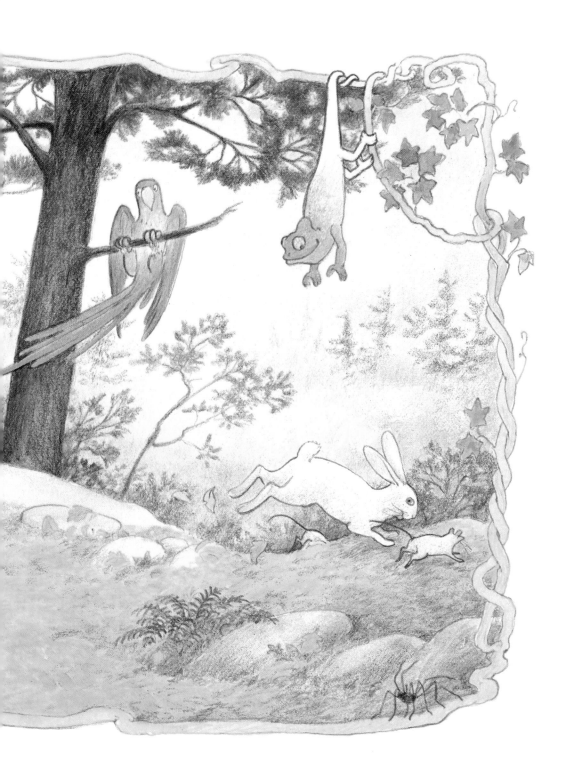

I want a green pet! Yes, I do.

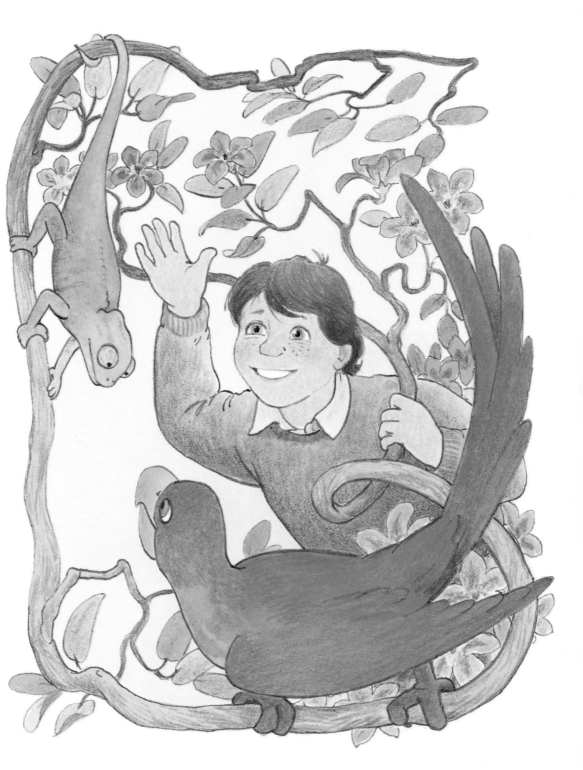

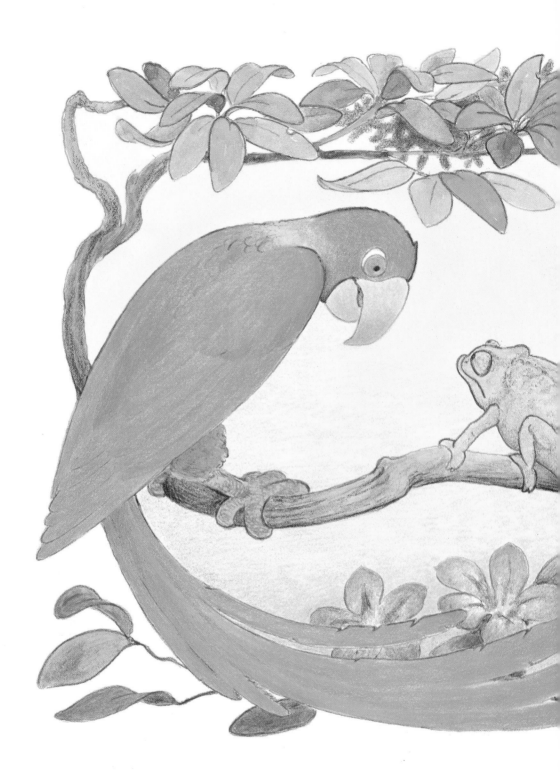

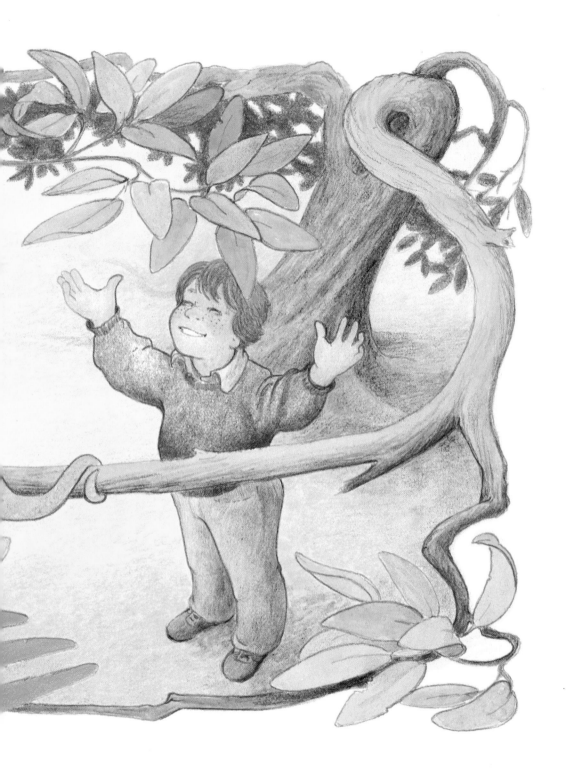

I want two green pets!

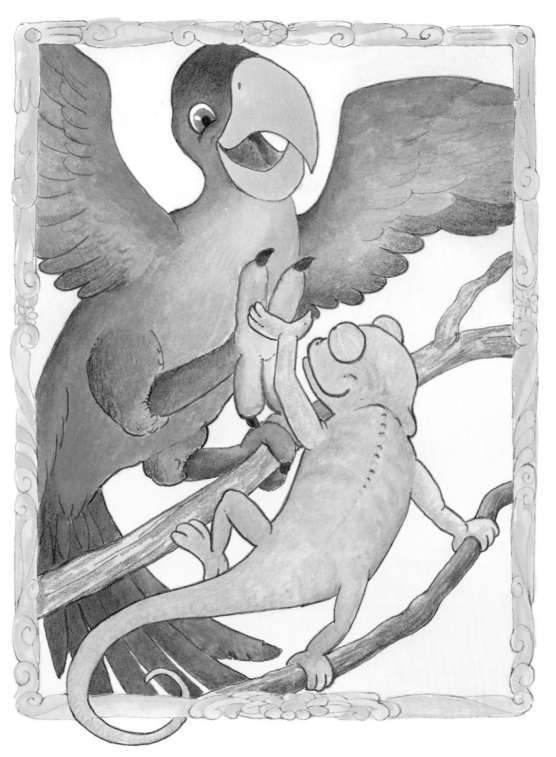

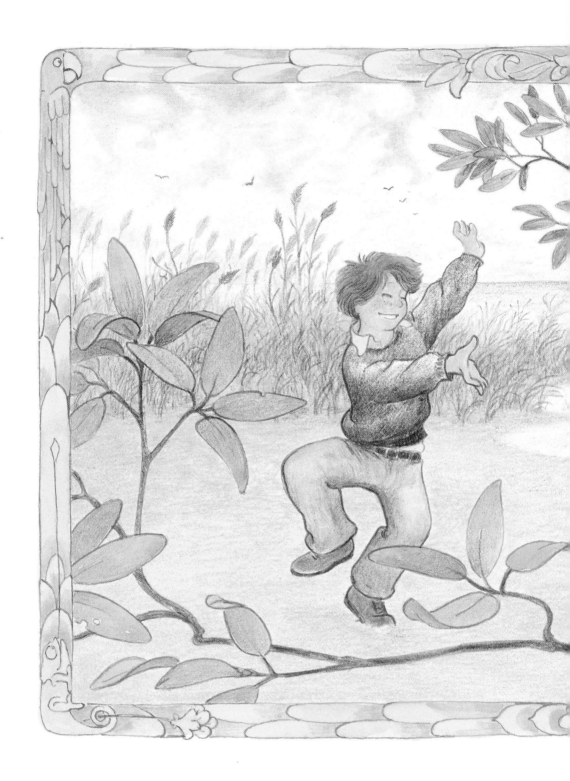

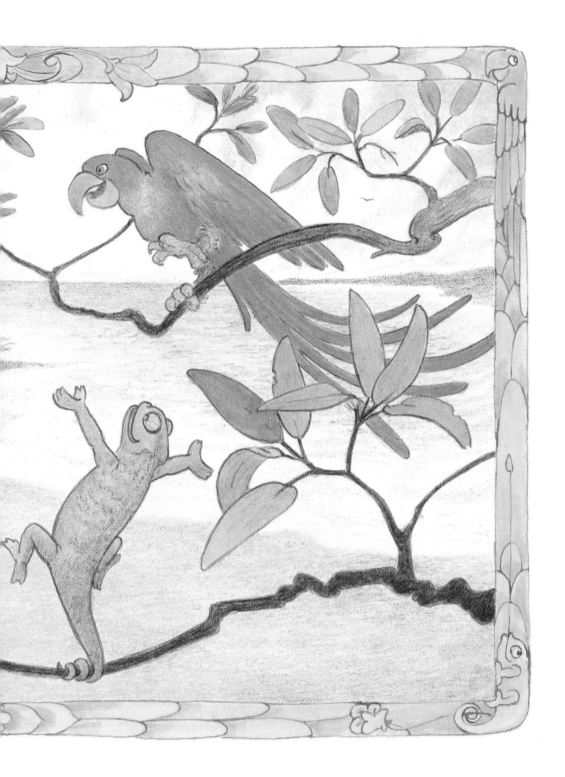

The End

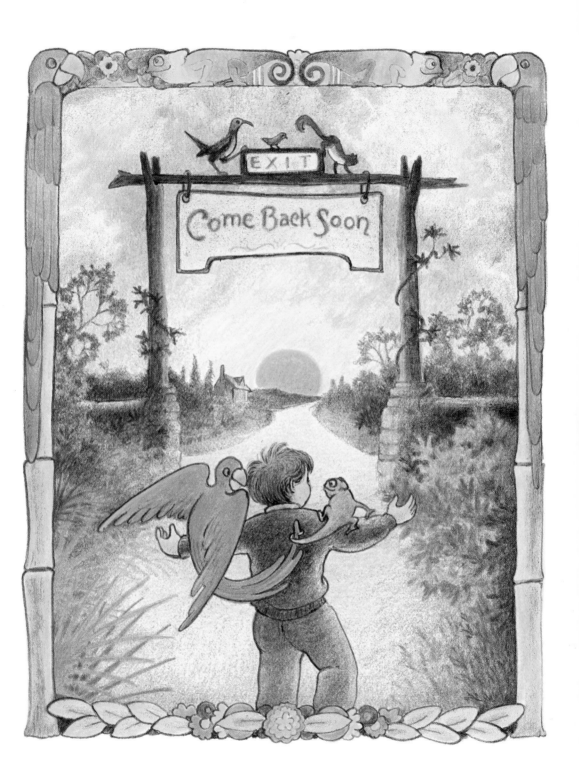